Bear Library
101 Governor's Place
Bear, DE 19701

W9-APH-284

For my mighty wonderful family,
from coast to coast—A. S. C.

For Dan and Becky—D. M.

SIMON & SCHUSTER BOOKS FOR YOUNG READERS
An imprint of Simon & Schuster Children's Publishing Division
1230 Avenue of the Americas, New York, New York 10020
Text copyright © 2018 by Alyssa Satin Capucilli
Illustrations copyright © 2018 by David Mottram
All rights reserved, including the right of reproduction in whole or in part in any form.
SIMON & SCHUSTER BOOKS FOR YOUNG READERS is a trademark of Simon & Schuster, Inc.
For information about special discounts for bulk purchases, please contact
Simon & Schuster Special Sales at 1-866-506-1949 or business@simonandschuster.com.
The Simon & Schuster Speakers Bureau can bring authors to your live event. For more information or to book an event,
contact the Simon & Schuster Speakers Bureau at 1-866-248-3049 or visit our website at www.simonspeakers.com.
Book design by Chloë Foglia
The text for this book was set in Chaloops, Stempel Garamond, and hand-lettered.
The illustrations for this book were rendered using watercolor and gouache and composed digitally.
Manufactured in China
1117 SCP
First Edition
2 4 6 8 10 9 7 5 3 1
CIP data for this book is available from the Library of Congress.
ISBN 978-1-4814-7681-2
ISBN 978-1-4814-7682-9 (eBook)

MIGHTY TUG

Written by

Alyssa Satin Capucilli

Illustrated by

David Mottram

A PAULA WISEMAN BOOK

Simon & Schuster Books for Young Readers

NEW YORK   LONDON   TORONTO   SYDNEY   NEW DELHI

Mighty Tug sings a wake-up tune,
to the sleepy skyscrapers beneath the yellow moon.

CLANG CLANG
CLANG CLANG
CLANG

All aboard!

Here I come, busy harbor.

Her lights flick on;
the waves start to play.
What will this little tugboat do today?

First Mighty Tug pulls a cargo ship
filled with bananas and fruits
to a waiting slip.

Then under the bridge
and around a sloop,
Mighty Tug tows a big barge too.

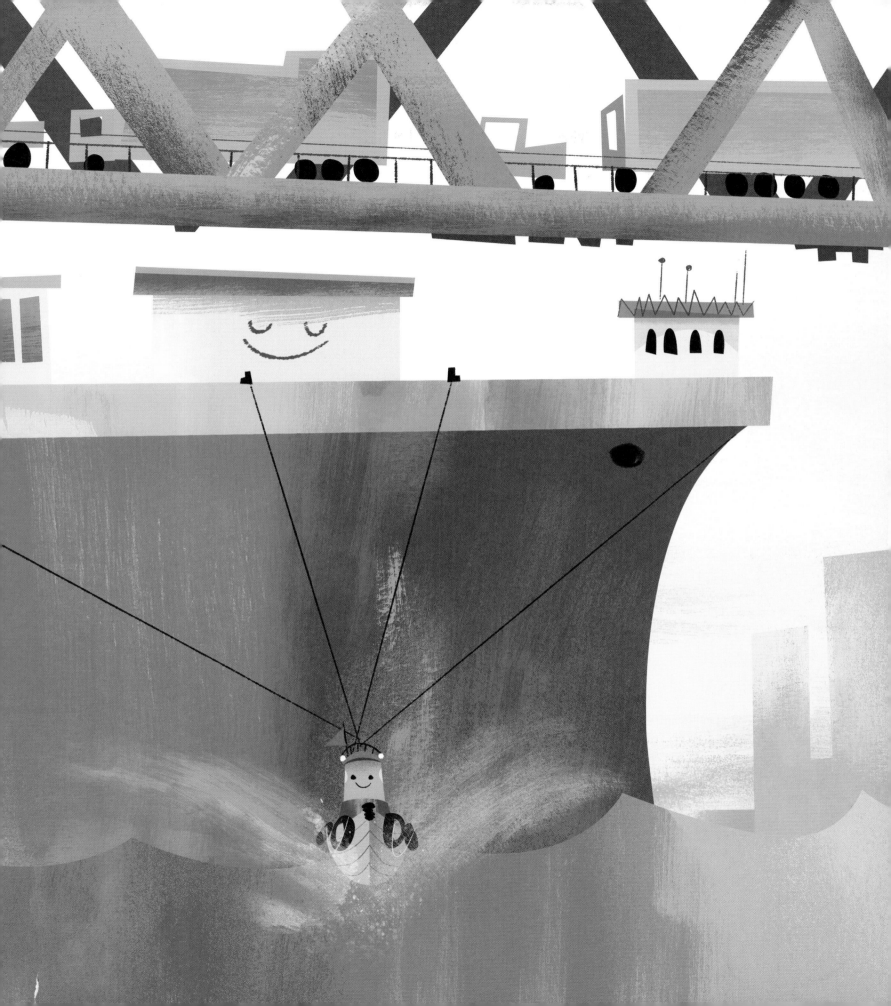

Waving her flag, to the dock and back out,
the tide comes with a tickle, rushing all about.

SPLISH SPLASH
SPLISH SPLASH

Steady she goes
in the busy, busy harbor.

The sun shines brightly;
the water's all aglow.
What now, little tugboat?
Which way will you go?

Down to the bay!
Rafts need a tug or two. . . .
With a hum and a whir,
Mighty Tug can do this, too.

Fishing boats signal,
and ferries call.
There goes the little tug. . . .

Heave ho and haul!

Small but oh so strong, she splashes toward shore,
where the pigeons peck and the seagulls soar!

VROOM
VROOM

What's next in the busy, busy harbor?

VROOM

Towering container ships,
filled to the brim
ask Mighty Tug,

"Will you guide us in?"

Around the gleaming channel,
   where the water's deep and wide,
      tall ships stretch their sails;
         Mighty Tug hugs their side.

Push-and-pulling across the harbor,

until the daylight slips away.

The sleepy sun calls,
"Time to end this tugboat's day!"

But wait! A speedy fireboat stacked with hoses and jugs cries out,

"Sound the alarm! Will you help us, Mighty Tug?"

Ready as ever, and oh so brave,
the mighty little tug leads the way across the waves!

RING RING RING RING RING RING

To the rescue in the busy, busy harbor.

BEEP BEEP BEEP BEEP

Full speed ahead in the busy, busy harbor.

All are safe in the busy, busy harbor.
With a wave of her flag, Mighty Tug turns away.
She's tired, but *so proud* of her busy harbor day.

There's a wink from Lady Liberty,
and a kiss from the fish.

Tucked in snug beneath the stars,
the little tug makes a wish . . .

Rest now, harbor, hush—not a peep,

Let the gentle waters hold you and rock you to sleep.

Tomorrow we'll meet to work and to play,

Tomorrow we'll share another busy harbor day.

CLANG CLANG
CLANG CLANG
CLANG

Sweet dreams, my busy, busy harbor.

E CAP $17.99
Mighty Tug.
Capucilli, Alyssa Satin, 1957-

01/10/2018   33910051406560

Bear Library
101 Governor's Place
Bear, DE 19701